THIS WALKER BOOK BELONGS TO:

To my parents

C.V.

First published 1990 by Walker Books Ltd
87 Vauxhall Walk, London SE11 5HJ

This edition published 1996

6 8 10 9 7 5

Text © 1990 Margaret Clark
Illustrations © 1990 Charlotte Voake

Printed in China

British Library Cataloguing in Publication Data:
a catalogue record for this book
is available from the British Library

ISBN 0-7445-3149-7

www.walkerbooks.co.uk

THE VERY BEST
of
AESOP'S
Fables

Retold by Margaret Clark

Illustrated by Charlotte Voake

WALKER BOOKS
AND SUBSIDIARIES
LONDON • BOSTON • SYDNEY

Contents

Foreword

I wish I could say that I had loved Aesop's Fables as a child, but in my memory they are identified for ever with those dauntingly worthy and solid editions of "children's classics" that were chosen by well-meaning adults in the 1930s with intent to teach rather than to entertain. Bound in tooled leather, meant to last a lifetime, they were so intimidating that nothing would have induced me to open books that so plainly declared they were "good for children".

Perhaps that's why the word "fable" has kept the connotation of "do-gooding" for me ever since. That's a shame, for poor Aesop—and no one seems to know exactly who he was—must have told his stories primarily to entertain, to hold the attention of his audience. Almost of secondary importance is the fact that the stories, though peopled by animals, are about human behaviour and how, in the end, most of us get our come-uppance if we concentrate too hard on our own concerns and don't think about others in the course of going about our daily life.

If we accept what the scholars tell us, Aesop was what we would now deem "under-privileged", if not handicapped: he was a slave, of legendary ugliness, who lived on the Greek island of Samos in the sixth century BC. The stories ascribed to him were not written down until about 200 years later. So whether he insisted on spelling out the morals underlying his stories we don't know. Charlotte Voake and I decided they were best left unsaid: if children understand and enjoy the stories as we have presented them, they will certainly appreciate the morals behind them. What we have tried to do is to dispel altogether the "preacherly" tone from the best of Aesop's shrewd and funny stories.

Margaret Clark

THE HARE and THE TORTOISE

A hare was one day making fun of a tortoise. "You are a slowcoach," he said. "You couldn't run if you tried."

"Don't you laugh at me," said the tortoise. "I bet that I could beat you in a race."

"Couldn't," replied the hare.

"Could," said the tortoise.

"All right," said the hare. "I'll race you. But I'll win, even with my eyes shut." They asked a passing fox to set them off.

"Ready, steady, go!" said the fox.

The hare went off at a great pace. He got so far ahead he decided he might as well stop for a rest. Soon he fell fast asleep. The tortoise came plodding along, never stopping for a moment. When the hare woke up, he ran as fast as he could to the finishing line...

9

But he was too late — the tortoise had already won the race.

THE CAT and THE MICE

A family of mice was being chased every day by a hungry cat.

"What are we going to do?" said Mother, as they all sat around her one evening.

Everyone had something to suggest, but the smallest mouse said, "If we hang a bell round his neck, then we shall hear him coming and we'll have time to get out of his way."

All the mice squealed in excitement and told the smallest mouse how clever he was.

Then the oldest mouse in the family spoke.

"That may sound a good idea," he said, "but tell me: which one of you is brave enough to go up to the cat and hang a bell round his neck?"

And why do you think none of them answered?

THE FOX and

There was a fox who just loved to make fun of other people. One day he invited a stork to dinner. "I have made some delicious soup specially for you,"

he said. But when they went to the table, the stork saw that the soup was in a very shallow dish and she could not drink a single drop with her long, pointed bill. The fox laughed when she tried. "So you don't like my soup," he jeered. "All the more for me!" And he lapped up the whole lot. The stork was so hurt by the fox's behaviour that she made up her mind to get her own back. "Do come to dinner with me," she said. "I know you are fond of soup, so I have made some specially for you."

THE STORK

The fox licked his lips, thinking how stupid the stork was. But when he came up to the stork's table, he saw that she had put the soup in a jug with a long, thin neck and his tongue could never reach it. "Tit for tat," snapped the stork in her prim voice. The fox went home hungry, with his tail between his legs.

THE BOY WHO CRIED WOLF

A boy was sent to look after a flock of sheep as they grazed near a village. It was raining, and he was bored, so he decided to play a trick on the villagers. "Wolf! Wolf!" he shouted as loud as he could. "There's a wolf attacking your sheep."

Out ran all the villagers, leaving whatever they were doing, to drive away the wolf. When they rushed into the field and found the sheep quite safe, the boy laughed and laughed.

The next day the same thing happened.

"Wolf! Wolf!" shouted the boy.
And when the villagers ran into
the field and again found everything
quiet, he laughed more than ever.
On the third day a wolf
really did come.
"Wolf! Wolf!" shouted the boy, as the
sheep ran wildly in all directions.
"Oh, please come quickly!"
But this time none of the villagers took
any notice, because they thought
he was only playing tricks,
as he had done before.

THE FOX
and
THE GRAPES

One day a fox, who was hot
and tired and very thirsty,
saw some fat, juicy grapes
hanging from a vine high above
his head. He stood on tiptoe and
stretched as high as he could,
but they were just out of reach.
Then he began to jump, for now he
wanted those grapes more
than anything else in the world.
But the higher he jumped, the
further away they seemed to be.
At last he was so tired he gave up. "I
don't care," he said crossly. "Those
grapes weren't ripe anyway."
(But of course he knew they were.)

THE LION & THE MOUSE

A lion was dozing in the shade
after a large meal,
when a mouse ran across his tummy.
The lion felt something tickling him, so he put out his paw
and picked up the little mouse, who squealed with terror.
"Oh, please don't eat me," said the mouse. "I'll make such a very
small mouthful. Let me go, and one day
I'll do you a good turn."

The lion laughed. "You! What could you ever do for me?"
But he wasn't hungry so he let the mouse go.

Some weeks later the mouse heard the
lion roaring with pain. The great king
had been caught by hunters and
was tied up with rope.

When the mouse saw this,
he started gnawing at the rope with his sharp little teeth.
It took him a long, long time, but at last the lion was free.
The mouse looked up and said, "There, you see!
You'd be in big trouble if it weren't for me."
Then the lion slunk away
without a word.

THE WOLF
and
HIS SHADOW

One day, when the sun was low in the sky, a wolf caught sight of an enormous shadow on the ground beside him. He looked all round, but there was no one else about.

"Why, that's _my_ shadow," said the wolf. "What a wonderful animal I must be! I've never even seen another animal as big as that. The lion calls himself king, but he's not nearly as big as I am. I'm going to be king from now on."

So the wolf strutted about, thinking of all the things he would do now he was king. He was so busy thinking about himself, he didn't even notice the lion, who suddenly sprang on him and swallowed him whole.

As the lion licked his lips, he said, "What a silly wolf! Everyone knows that sometimes your shadow is big, sometimes it's small, and sometimes you have no shadow at all."

THE TOWN MOUSE
and
THE COUNTRY MOUSE

There was once a country mouse who lived in a field and a town mouse who lived behind the skirting-board of a large kitchen. The town mouse went to spend a holiday with the country mouse, and on the first evening they sat down together for a supper of grains of barley and ears of corn.

The town mouse did not like this food at all and said to her friend, "My poor dear, this is no life for you! At my house there are much better things to eat, and if you come and stay you can share them with me."

So they set off at once, without even finishing their meal. When they reached the town, they went into the house, and the town mouse showed the country mouse all round the kitchen, which was filled with cheese and chutney, jam and honey, cake and jelly, and lots of other good things.

The country mouse had never seen anything like it before, and she and her friend were just about to start on this feast when the cook came in through the door. "Quick!" said the town mouse. "Into that hole in the skirting-board!"

The country mouse was very frightened and uncomfortable hiding in the hole with her friend.

When all was quiet, the two mice came out again and once more started to eat. Again, the door opened, in came the cook, and again they had to rush for the safety of their hole.

This time the country mouse decided she had had enough. "I'm off home, my friend," she said. "You can keep your cheese, your honey, your cake and your jelly. I'd rather enjoy my barley and corn in peace, without running into a hole every five minutes!"

And she went back

to her comfortable home in the country.

THE WOLF and THE HERON

A wolf got a bone stuck in his throat. It hurt so much when he tried to swallow that he went to look for someone who could take it out. Luckily he met a heron and when he saw its long, pointed beak he knew this was just the thing to pick out the bone. So he asked the heron nicely if it would help him. The heron stopped and thought for a minute.

"What will you give me if I put my head in your mouth?"

"There'll be a big reward," gasped the wolf.

The heron put its head inside the wolf's mouth
and gently pulled the bone from his throat.

The wolf, now feeling much better, thanked
the heron and went on his way.

"Hey!" called the heron.

"What about my reward?"

"You've got it," said the wolf. "From now on you can boast to everyone that you put your head inside a wolf's mouth and didn't get it bitten off."

THE HEN and THE FOX

A fox went into a hen-house looking for something to eat. There, high above his head on a perch, sat a large fat hen. "My dear girl," he called up to her, "you don't look very well today. Why don't you come down here so that I can feel your pulse and take your temperature?"

The hen knew perfectly well what the fox wanted. "I certainly haven't felt very well since you came in," she said, "but I'm sure I would feel much worse if you came any closer. I'm better up here, thank you very much."

THE MILLER,
HIS SON
and THEIR DONKEY

A miller was driving his donkey to market. His young son trudged along behind him. "How silly you are!" said a girl they passed on the road. "Why make your son walk when he could ride on the donkey?"

"What a good idea!" said the miller, and he lifted his son on to the donkey's back.

The miller went on driving the donkey but soon he began to feel very hot.

"How silly you are!" said a friend of the miller's who came up behind them. "You spoil that son of yours. Why don't <u>you</u> ride the donkey and make him walk?"

"What a good idea!" said the miller, lifting the boy off the donkey's back and mounting it himself. The boy soon began to trail far behind.

"How selfish you are!" said a woman sitting by the roadside. "Why don't you let the boy ride with you?"

"What a good idea!" said the miller, lifting the boy up beside him.

After a while the donkey was so tired it could hardly put one foot in front of the other.

"How silly you are!" said a traveller, passing them. "If you ride that donkey all the way to market, it will be worn out when you get there, and no one will buy it. You'd better carry it and give it a rest."

"What a good idea!" said the miller. He got off the donkey and lifted his son down. Then they tied the donkey's legs together and carried it upside down on a pole. The donkey was very frightened. It kicked and struggled so much that, just as they were passing over a bridge, its ropes broke and it fell into the river. And they never saw it again.